I0783745

Up to the Sky

Dee Gee Simms

Dedication

This book is dedicated to my three children: a sweetie, a smartie, and a softie, and my five delightful grandchildren.

Thanks to my oldest grandchild for asking about their uncle.

Kai loves Uncle JJ
Uncle JJ loves Kai too

Together with their playfulness
There's much that they can do

Kai loves Uncle JJ's bike
Kai sees it near and far

JJ plays Kai music
When he presses on a star

Kai plays Uncle JJ's drums
Sticks pointing way up high

Uncle JJ is so tall
He lifts Kai to the sky

Of all the things that they can do
They love each other best

That's why one day when JJ left
Kai felt sad in the chest

JJ seven? Kai would ask
In that cute childlike way

Yes Kai, JJ is in heaven
Grandma she would say

Then one day in Grandma's car
They drove over railroad tracks

Where's the train? Where is JJ?
Kai decided to ask

Well JJ's on a train I know
But we cannot see where

Maybe if we look real hard
We'll see it in the air

Up to the sky and far beyond
The train drives out of sight

Do you know someone on that train?
They're riding with JJ tonight!

Hi JJ Hi Grandpa Hi Tonka
Hi Pumpkin

Hi ________   Hi ________
Hi ________   Hi ________

The End

www.ingramcontent.com/pod-product-compliance
Lightning Source LLC
Chambersburg PA
CBHW040845010826
48978CB00012BB/907